THE BOY WHO COULD DO WHAT HE LIKED

This book belongs to:

I celebrated World Book Day 2016 with this
brilliant gift from my local Bookseller and
HarperCollins Children's Books.

Also by David Baddiel

THE PARENT AGENCY

THE PERSON CONTROLLER

This book has been specially written and published for World Book Day 2016. For further information, visit www.worldbookday.com

World Book Day in the UK and Ireland is made possible by generous sponsorship from National Book Tokens, participating publishers, authors, illustrators and booksellers.

Booksellers who accept the £1* World Book Day Book Token bear the full cost of redeeming it.

World Book Day, World Book Night and Quick Reads are annual initiatives designed to encourage everyone in the UK and Ireland – whatever your age – to read more and discover the joy of books and reading for pleasure.

World Book Night is a celebration of books and reading for adults and teens on 23rd April, which sees book gifting and celebrations in thousands of communities around the country: www.worldbooknight.org

Quick Reads provides brilliant short new books by bestselling authors to engage adults in reading: www.quickreads.org.uk

*€1.50 in Ireland

First published iin Great Britain by *HarperCollins Children's Books* in 2016
HarperCollins *Children's Books* is a division of HarperCollins*Publishers* Ltd,
1 London Bridge Street London, SE1 9GF

The HarperCollins website address is: www.harpercollins.co.uk

1

ISBN: 978-00-0-816488-1

David Baddiel asserts the moral right to be identified as the author of
the work. Jim Field asserts the moral right to be identified as the
illustrator of the work.

Printed and bound in England by Clays Ltd, St Ives plc

MIX
Paper from
responsible sources
FSC **FSC™ C007454**
www.fsc.org

FSC™ is a non-profit international organisation established to promote
the responsible management of the world's forests. Products carrying the
FSC label are independently certified to assure consumers that they come
from forests that are managed to meet the social, economic and
ecological needs of present and future generations,
and other controlled sources.

Find out more about HarperCollins and the environment at
www.harpercollins.co.uk/green

THE BOY WHO COULD DO WHAT HE LIKED

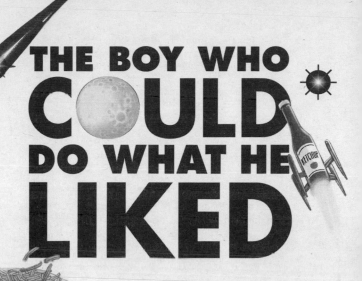

DAVID BADDIEL

Illustrated by Jim Field

HarperCollins *Children's Books*

To the real Mrs Stokes...

PART 1

CHAPTER 1
3.32pm

Alfie Moore had a routine. To be honest, he had a *lot* of routines. He had a waking-up routine, a getting-dressed routine, a cleaning-his-teeth-in-the-morning routine, a breakfast routine, a clearing-up-after-breakfast routine, a getting-his-schoolbag-ready routine, a checking-he-had-everything-before-he-left-the-house routine, a walking-to-and-from-school routine, a having-tea routine, a clearing-up-after-tea routine, a homework routine, a limited-amount-of-TV routine, a bath routine, a cleaning-his-teeth-in-the-evening routine (which, to be fair, was pretty similar to his cleaning-his-teeth-in-the-morning routine), a getting-undressed-and-putting-pyjamas-on routine and a going-to-bed routine.

Alfie was eleven and the routines had all been worked out by his dad, Stephen. Each one was precisely written out, listing all the things he had to do, and the times he had do them by, on pieces of paper pinned up on different walls of his house. For example, the waking-up and getting-dressed routines were on his bedroom wall, along with the getting-undressed-and-putting-pyjamas-on and going-to-bed routines, only on a different piece of paper (placed very neatly next to the first one).

But Alfie never needed to look at those pieces of paper because he knew all his routines by heart. Plus, he wore two watches, one on each wrist (one digital and one analogue, both given to him by his dad) to make sure he always knew the time. As a result, he was never late for school, always knew what clothes to wear, was never tired from going to bed late and always got all his homework done.

Alfie was perfectly happy. The routines made his life work very, very well; it only *wasn't* operating under a routine when he was asleep, although Alfie didn't really know about that because he never seemed to have any dreams.

Alfie's routines did, of course, involve his dad and his stepmother, Jenny. His parents were there at exactly the right times to prepare his tea, to help him with his homework, to kiss him on the top of his head when the back of his head hit the pillow, as it always did at 8.35pm on weekdays and

9.35pm on weekends. But every so often Alfie's parents did go out, to dinner parties and other things that they said they liked, but often came back from crosser and more miserable than they were before they went out. That could mean a disruption to Alfie's evening routines.

Luckily, they had a babysitter who was completely up to speed with how Alfie lived his life. Her name was Stasia and she was Lithuanian. If anything, she was even more efficient than Alfie's dad at making sure Alfie stuck to his regular timetable.

Stasia would arrive, promptly, at 6pm and everything would run smoother than smooth with Alfie's having-tea routine, his clearing-up-after-tea routine, his homework routine, his limited-amount-of-TV routine, his bath routine, his pretty-similar-to-the-cleaning-his-teeth-in-the-morning-cleaning-his-teeth-in-the-evening routine, his getting-undressed-and-putting-pyjamas-on routine and his going-to-bed routine.

But then, one day, Alfie came back from school to find his stepmum, Jenny, video-calling Stasia on her smartphone. He wanted to interrupt her and tell her all about his science class, which he had really liked that day because they'd been doing space travel, but he could see that she was preoccupied.

"But what are we going to do?" his stepmum was saying. "We've got a dinner party tonight. It's Stephen's boss. I really don't think we can cancel."

Alfie's stepmum, it should be said, was not quite as concerned about the routines as Alfie's dad. In fact, if anything, she was a bit worried that Alfie was being teased at school for his punctuality and his always-having-his-homework-doneness: she thought she'd heard a boy called Freddie Barnes shout: "BORING, BORING ALFIE!" at him in the playground.

But she knew the routines had started soon

after Alfie's biological mum had died and that they had made day-to-day life much easier while Stephen was a single dad. And, even though Stephen wasn't a single dad any more, he seemed to want to stick with the routines and Jenny didn't like challenging him about how he had decided to bring up his son.

"I am sorry, Mrs Moore," said Stasia from the phone screen. "I cannot help it. My family needs me. I must catch a plane at 7.30."

Jenny shook her head. "How heavy *is* this pig?"

"Was. The pig is dead."

"Dead? Running into your mother killed the pig?"

"No. Because she broke my mother's leg, the pig has been destroyed." There was a short pause. "Although we will eat her later." There was another short pause. "The pig. Not my mother."

"OK…" said Jenny. "Fine. Of course. I understand. Go. We'll… find someone else."

But when she clicked off and looked up, Alfie could tell she was worried. And *he* was worried too because they'd never had any other babysitters, apart from his grandparents, and both sets lived too far away to reach his house in time.

Who were they going to get to look after him?

CHAPTER 2
5.30pm

The situation got worse when Alfie's dad arrived home and discovered that Stasia had to fly back to Lithuania to deal with her emergency pig-induced crisis. Going to his boss's dinner party was *non-negotiable*, he said. Alfie wasn't sure what non-negotiable meant, but it seemed to suggest that his parents were going to go out whatever happened. He started to think they might just leave him home alone or, worse, take him with them and then he'd have to talk to grown-ups about management consultancy, which is what his dad did, and Alfie had even less idea what that actually meant than non-negotiable.

"There must be someone else we can call," said Jenny. "What about the next-door neighbours?"

"They're away on holiday," replied Alfie's dad.

Alfie, not really liking it when his dad and stepmum got frantic, went over to the other side of the living room where there was a chest of drawers. Inside the top drawer there were lots of bits of paper, including some of the bits of paper that his dad had first drawn up his routines on. Alfie liked to look at these sometimes to see how his routines had changed as he had got older.

"OK," said Jenny. "What about the other side? Mr Nichols…"

"Are you serious? He stands all day at the lights on the High Street, directing traffic with a spoon."

Jenny nodded. "You're right. Bad idea." She sat down, took out her phone and started tapping. "We could call an agency…"

"No, Jenny."

"No?"

"No. I don't want someone we've never met. How could we trust them to be on top of everything?"

"On top of every… what thing?"

Stephen looked at her like she was mad. "The routines, Jenny. Alfie's *routines*."

Alfie's stepmum stopped tapping. She put the phone down and sighed.

"Then I'm out of ideas," she said.

Alfie's dad put his head in his hands. "What are we going to do?" he said, sounding muffled.

"What about this?" suggested Alfie.

He held out a small card that he had found under some of the bits of paper in the chest of drawers. It had gone slightly yellow with age, but you could still make out a picture of flowers on it. In the middle of the flowers were printed the words:

MRS STOKES
BABYSITTER

and a phone number. On the back of the card someone had written, in biro:

in case of emergencies

His dad looked at the card. He turned it over. He seemed, for some reason, shocked by it.

"Um… well, I guess… we could try her." He showed the card to Jenny.

"Do you know her…?" said Jenny, surprised.

"No, I don't think we ever used her, but…" He turned the card over so that Jenny could see the writing on the back.

Jenny squinted at it. "Is that…?"

"Yes."

Jenny thought for a while. "Well then, I guess it must be OK. Although, looking at the state of that card, I think Mrs Stokes might be quite old now."

Jenny was right. When Alfie first saw Mrs Stokes, he didn't think he'd ever seen anyone so ancient. She made his oldest grandparent, Grandpa Bernie, look like a member of a boy band. She had a Zimmer frame, two hearing aids and – although Alfie didn't know how tall she might have been before – seemed to have shrunk with age to the size of a munchkin. And it took her so long to walk up the drive that, by the time she was actually inside the house, Alfie wondered if it was too late for his parents to go out.

How on earth, he thought, *is she going to look after me? And, more importantly, make sure I get through all my routines?*

CHAPTER 3
6.00pm

The first problem, in fact, was making Mrs Stokes understand what a routine was.

"Shoe-bean?" she said loudly to Stephen. "Your son has a bean in his shoe? Baked or haricot?"

"No," said Stephen, sighing. He bent down to her ear, which Alfie could see was very small and poking out of her extremely white hair. She was sitting in the kitchen, drinking a cup of tea that Jenny had made, and into which Mrs Stokes had put a seemingly endless amount of sugar.

"ROO-TINE. I said I'd like Alfie, if possible, to stick to his usual *routine*…"

"Oh dear, dear, dear," said Mrs Stokes, looking with concern at Alfie. "I'm so sorry."

"Pardon me?" said Stephen.

"That's all right, love," said Mrs Stokes. "I'm a bit deaf myself." She pulled Stephen's face down by his ear and shouted into it: **"I'M SO SORRY!!"**

"*Ow!*" said Stephen, pulling away and rubbing his ear. "What about?"

"Your son having to have a *poo-team*," said Mrs Stokes. "I've never heard of that before in such a young person. So, where are they? How many people normally help him go to the toilet?"

Alfie's dad frowned and whispered to Jenny: "I *really* don't know if we should go out and leave Alfie with her."

"Why are you bothering to whisper?" said Jenny.

Stephen looked at Mrs Stokes, who was happily smiling at him. "Good point," he said in a normal voice. "Maybe I should just call it off after all."

"Well, OK, phone your boss and—"

But, as she was saying this, Stephen's phone rang.

"It's him," he said, looking stressed. "He'll be asking why we're not there already. Pre-dinner drinks started at six…" And he dashed off into the hallway, apologising to his boss in hushed tones. Jenny exchanged a glance with Alfie.

"Mrs Stokes," said Jenny, crouching down. Alfie noticed that the old lady was dressed a little bit like the Queen – all in green, with a necklace of pearls – but as if the Queen bought her clothes at Oxfam. "Alfie doesn't have *a poo-team*. He has *routines*."

"Oh, I see. Where did you get them from, Topman?"

Now it was Jenny's turn to frown. "Sorry, not quite with you, Mrs Stokes."

"His *new jeans*. I prefer Primark myself." She took a sip from her cup. "Lovely spot of tea. Can I have another?"

Alfie watched all this with increasing horror. He looked at his stepmum, but she was writing something down on her phone. She held it out to Mrs Stokes. It said:

MRS STOKES, WOULD YOU MIND PLEASE SWITCHING YOUR HEARING AIDS ON?

The babysitter seemed to consider this for a while. Eventually, she said: "Well, OK. I don't know why you think that's important seeing as we've been having such a lovely chat. But you're the boss. Hold on a minute."

She reached into her ears with both hands and made a series of tiny adjustments to the bits of plastic inside. Her fingers were stiff and Alfie became concerned that she might get them stuck in there. The whole process probably took about three minutes, but appeared to Alfie to last at least an hour.

Suddenly, there was the most terrible high-pitched squealing.

"WHAT'S THAT NOISE?!" shouted Alfie.

"I DON'T KNOW!" replied Jenny loudly. "IT SOUNDS LIKE MY OLD *JESUS AND MARY CHAIN* RECORDS!"

"IT SEEMS TO BE COMING FROM… HER!!" said Alfie, pointing to Mrs Stokes.

"Sorry, dearies," said the old lady. "If I switch them both on together, they do tend to feedback a bit. Hold on a mo."

At this point, Stephen came back into the room. "WHAT'S THAT AWFUL NOISE?!" he shouted.

"IT'S MRS STOKES'S HEARING AIDS!" yelled Alfie.

"WHAT?"

"MRS STOKES'S HEARING AIDS! THE THINGS SHE PUTS IN HER EARS TO HELP HER HEAR!!"

"I CAN'T HEAR YOU!" Stephen bellowed.

Mrs Stokes herself seemed impervious to the sound, fiddling and fine-tuning inside her ears again.

"DO WE HAVE TO GO TO THE DINNER PARTY?" shouted Jenny.

Stephen made a face, meaning, *Yes, probably – but I'm still not happy with Mrs 2,000 Years Old here.* (Alfie was quite good at reading his dad's expressions.)

Jenny thought for a moment and then passed Stephen the card, the old one with Mrs Stokes's name on it and the words *in case of emergencies*. She raised her eyebrows meaningfully. Alfie watched his dad look at the card for a while and then come to some sort of a decision.

"OK," said Stephen. "Fine." He turned towards the old lady. "MRS STOKES! MRS STOKES! WE'RE GOING OUT NOW!!!"

Mrs Stokes nodded and smiled, oblivious to the fact that the feedback from her hearing aids seemed, if anything, to be getting both louder and higher pitched.

"SO, I'D LIKE ALFIE TO STICK TO HIS USUAL ROUTINE IF POSSIBLE.

AND DEFINITELY IN BED BY…"

The feedback suddenly stopped. Which meant that when Stephen finished his sentence by saying,

"…9.35PM!!!",

it was much too loud.

Mrs Stokes sat back in her chair and said: "Blimey. No need to shout, dear!"

Stephen shut his eyes and took a deep breath. "I was saying," he said, "that I'd like Alfie to be in bed by 9.35pm if possible. And, before that, to stick to his usual routines."

"Oh. That's no problem," said Mrs Stokes. "Hang on, I'll make a note of it."

She opened her handbag, which smelt so much of mothballs that moths from miles around must have flown away, terrified. Nonetheless, Stephen and Jenny and Alfie breathed a sigh of relief as they watched her write.

"His... usual... blue cream," she said, holding up her pad and reading out the words, which were written in neat, if shaky, capitals. "What is it, a kind of pudding? I like Spotted Dick myself."

CHAPTER 4
6.15pm

Eventually, though, Alfie's parents managed to make Mrs Stokes understand what a routine was. Which meant that Stephen and Jenny could finally leave the house.

They were just about to go out of the front door when his dad paused for a moment by a picture in the hallway.

It was a painting that had been done by Alfie's mum – his real mum – of the sea. It wasn't one of those nice but boring ones, like people sell at craft fairs, of some cottages by the coast. His dad had told Alfie – who was too little to remember – that one of the things his mum had always wanted to do before she died was swim with dolphins. She never got to do that so instead she had painted this amazing picture, swirling with colour and movement and adventure, of what the sea might look like if you were rushing through it underwater.

Alfie had seen it so often he now forgot it was there. But, just at this moment, his dad was staring at it, like the painting had put him into a trance.

"Dad," said Alfie, shaking his father out of it. "Are you sure about… going out tonight?"

Unexpectedly, he heard a voice from the small toilet beneath the stairs.

"Don't worry! It'll be fine! I'll make sure everything's all right here, you'll see!" Mrs Stokes opened the door a little and peeked out at Stephen and Jenny. "You go! You *need* to go! You definitely *need* to go!"

And she shut the door again.

Jenny and Stephen exchanged glances. Stephen crouched down and put his hand on Alfie's shoulder. "To be honest, Alfie, I'm *not* entirely sure. But here's the thing: if you just stick to your routines, everything will be fine."

Alfie looked into his dad's eyes, to see if he was telling the truth. Which was quite hard as they kept on looking off to the side, towards the painting, again.

"What do you think, Jenny?" said Alfie.

Jenny opened her mouth to answer – possibly even to disagree with Stephen a little, from the expression on her face – but Alfie's dad said: "Alfie. Let's not discuss it now. We *really* have to get going. And besides – especially if you're going to be asleep by 9.35pm! – you need to be getting on with your having-tea routine. You're already…" he checked his watch, "seven minutes and forty-three seconds late laying the table."

Alfie checked his watches. His dad was

right. He nodded and turned back slowly towards the kitchen.

"Seven minutes and forty-*five* seconds!" said his dad from behind him.

"Oh, come on, Stephen," said Jenny. "We're already late ourselves now!!"

"Oh no!" said Stephen, running out of the door.

CHAPTER 5
6.35pm

Alfie decided to make the best of it. He went and sat at the table, with his plate and knife and fork and glass of water all ready.

The trouble was that Mrs Stokes – who, according to the having-tea routine, was meant to get Alfie's meal out of the oven for him – wasn't with him. She was still in the toilet. She'd been there, Alfie realised, for quite an alarming length of time. He would have been more concerned were it not for the number of strange groaning noises she was making. He'd rather not have heard those sounds, but at least they convinced him that she wasn't – well – dead.

Finally, he heard a flush, followed about two minutes later by the sight of his babysitter humping her Zimmer frame down the hall.

"Mrs Stokes!" said Alfie. "It's Broccoli Bake for tea today! Jenny will have left it in the oven, so maybe, if I help you with your walking frame, you can—"

But Mrs Stokes just carried on towards the living room. Alfie sat there for a bit, not knowing what to do. He was shaken out of his reverie by the sight of a boy on a bike flashing past the kitchen window: a very familiar boy on a very familiar bike.

Oh no, thought Alfie.

"HEY!" shouted Freddie Barnes (for it was he), turning round and cycling back in front of the window. "IT'S ALFIE! BORING, BORING ALFIE!!"

Yes, Freddie Barnes *did* sometimes shout

that at Alfie, just as Jenny had feared.

After a little while saying the words "Boring, Boring Alfie" over and over again whilst laughing and pointing – which must have got dull fairly quickly, seeing as he was on his own with no other bullies to share this with – Freddie cycled off.

Alfie shook his head, got down from the table and went through into the living room where Mrs Stokes was sitting in an armchair, watching *Strictly Come Dancing* on TV. She looked completely engrossed.

"Er… Mrs Stokes?" said Alfie. "It's time for my tea. Well, actually…" he added, checking his watches, "…we're already a bit over. We should have been plated up eleven minutes ago. But anyway… you're meant to… bring me my tea."

"Yes, dear," said Mrs Stokes, without moving her eyes from the TV. "Just do what you like."

Alfie frowned. "Pardon?"

"I said, just do what you like."

Alfie wasn't sure how to take this. "But… you're meant to bring me my tea. Then, in the next fifteen minutes, I'm supposed to eat it. Then I clear up, bring my plate and cutlery and glass over to the sink and help you load the dishwasher. That's scheduled to take between six and nine minutes, depending on the size of the meal. Broccoli Bake should be at the lower end of that, I think, which is good because we're already running late."

"Yes, dear," said Mrs Stokes. "Absolutely. Just do what you like." And she turned the volume up on the TV.

Alfie didn't know what to do. So he ran round the house – back into the kitchen, upstairs to his bedroom, stopping on the landing to go into the bathroom, and then back down into the living room. He collected all the bits of paper from all the various walls and then handed them in a neat pile to Mrs Stokes.

"Mrs Stokes!" he said. "These are my evening routines. My having-tea routine, my clearing-up-after-tea routine, my homework routine, my limited-amount-of-TV routine, my bath routine, my cleaning-my-teeth-in-the-evening routine—"

"Is that very different from your cleaning-your-teeth-in-the-morning routine?" said Mrs Stokes.

"Er… no, they *are* pretty similar" said Alfie, slightly surprised that she'd heard what he'd been saying. "Anyway, there's also my getting-undressed-and-putting-pyjamas-on routine and my going-to-bed routine!"

"That's nice, love," said Mrs Stokes.

"No, but you don't understand," said Alfie desperately. "We're already…" he looked at both wrists, "…fourteen minutes late with having-tea. That means all the other routines will be fourteen minutes behind schedule. Unless we can make up some time, maybe on homework… or I guess I could have a shorter bath… But we need to get started!"

"All right, dear," said Mrs Stokes, handing all the pieces of paper back to Alfie. "You get on with it. *Just do what you like!*"

CHAPTER 6
6.49pm

Alfie remembered what his dad had said: *just stick to your routines*. It was clearly no good trying to get Mrs Stokes involved, so Alfie decided to get on with it on his own. He took all the paper routines and laid them out in front of him at the kitchen table. He didn't, after all, need a grown-up to help him through them, did he?

Well, unfortunately, yes. The first one, for example. The one that he was already fourteen – no, sixteen now – minutes behind for. Theoretically, he could do having-tea himself. But that meant going very off limits in the way the routines were meant to work. He was supposed to be in place, having laid the table, by 6.30pm. His stepmum, or Stasia, would then bring him tea. For him to bring *himself* tea confused everything. Not least because his tea was in the oven, on quite a hot plate, and he knew he wasn't supposed to get hot stuff out of the oven. That was definitely a grown-up's job.

There was one upside to all this: even though he'd accepted that it was always what he had for tea on a Saturday night, secretly Alfie didn't really like Broccoli Bake. He thought about getting something else, but when he looked in the cupboard most of the tins and packages in there contained stuff that needed cooking. Which he also couldn't do on his own.

And time was ticking by. He really needed to get on to his *next* routine, clearing-up-after-tea. But this presented both a practical problem and a philosophical one. Could he clear up after tea when he hadn't actually *had* any (that was the philosophical one)? He could clear the table, and bring his plate, glass and cutlery to the sink, but he hadn't used them, so did they need to be cleaned? And anyway he didn't know how to switch the dishwasher on; a grown-up had to do that (this was the practical problem).

Then, after that, there was homework. It was science – a whole essay he was meant to write, about the difference between mammals and marine animals... *tonight*. He needed a grown-up to help him with that too. Next on the list was a limited-amount-of-TV and he couldn't do that either because Mrs Stokes was sitting in front of the telly.

Alfie didn't want to go any further down the schedule because, if he couldn't get the next four tasks done, there was just no point. He simply wouldn't be sticking to his routines.

Which was what his dad had told him he had to do.

Alfie felt a rising panic in his throat. He knew, at some level, that his world was falling apart. He'd started to sweat and quite a large part of him wanted to cry, which he hadn't done for ages, not since his mum died. The feeling in his throat got worse and a shout came out that was half a scream. It might have been wordless, but it wasn't. It was two words.

"MRS STOKES!!!!!"

It was a last attempt to get the old lady to come and do her bit to make the routines happen.

"YES, DEAR!!" Her voice came
through, crackly as ever, from the living room.

"I DON'T KNOW WHAT TO DO!" shouted Alfie.

This, undoubtedly, was playing into Mrs Stokes's hands. "OH WELL!" she shouted, *"JUST DO WHAT YOU LIKE!!"*

Just do what you like? thought Alfie. *Are you going to say that over and over again? Just do what you like just do what you like just do what you like just do what you like!!!!*

"ALL RIGHT THEN!" Alfie shouted, thinking of time ticking away and his routines slipping past. He held his hands up in exasperation.

"I'LL JUST DO WHAT I LIKE!!"

And suddenly he noticed – because his hands were up in the air – that both his watches had stopped.

END OF PART 1

INTERLUDE

"As I'm sure you know, there's a lot of *talk* in our business about doing things *differently* – what people call *out of the box ideas*. But really, with management consultancy, it's all about sticking to what you *know*. Frankly, there is a box, and we've got to put the right things into it before we start thinking about everything *outside* of the box that might be… that might be…"

"Also put into the box?"

"Yes. Thank you, Juliana. We have to know what's *meant* to be in the box before we put stuff from *outside* the box into the box that's not *supposed* to be in there."

Stephen's boss, Trevor McNade – we could just call him Trevor, but he was one of those people who always seemed to demand a surname too – had been talking like this, about *boxes* and *ideas*, while emphasising certain words seemingly at random, for a while. Stephen and Jenny were in a circle of people standing round him, in his very grand living room, under his very grand chandelier. Everyone was holding champagne glasses and nodding. *Really* nodding.

Suddenly, though, Jenny stopped nodding.

"Sorry, Trevor…" – she wanted to say Trevor McNade, but she managed, just, to keep it to Trevor – "…but surely the whole point of thinking *outside* the box is that the stuff you think of – that's outside the box – well, it never goes in the box."

There was a short silence, during which Trevor McNade adjusted his tie, fiddled with his glasses and his suit buttons, and frowned at

Jenny. The elegant woman next to him – Juliana – whispered, "Stephen Moore's wife, sir," into his ear.

Stephen glared at Jenny. Jenny mouthed, *What*?

"What do you mean…" said Trevor McNade, "…*never goes in the box*?"

"Well, outside the box means… y'know… outside the box. So the expression refers to ideas and thoughts that are so unusual that we basically have to throw the box away."

Jenny laughed nervously as she said this. No one else joined in. Trevor McNade stared at her, like she was mad, for about a minute – but it felt much longer – and then started talking about something else. At which point Stephen made a furious head gesture to Jenny to meet him in Trevor McNade's very grand hallway.

"What?" said Jenny, out loud this time.

"Come on, darling. You know why we're

here," said Stephen, looking over her shoulder at the dining room, where guests were starting to sit down for dinner.

"To agree with everything Trevor McNade says?"

"Yes. Basically."

Jenny sighed. "OK. I'm sorry. Let's get it over with. Do you want to call the babysitter and check everything's all right before we begin dinner?"

Stephen nodded and took out his phone. Then suddenly, down Trevor McNade's long and (obviously) very grand staircase, came a young boy wearing a suit and tie and glasses – a suit and tie and glasses very similar to, but a little smaller than, Trevor McNade's.

"Would you *please* get out of my *way*?" said the boy.

"Sorry," said Stephen, moving aside.

"Ridiculous, you *people* cluttering up the *hallway*. My father *specifically* asked me to join his guests in the dining room at 6.49pm as we *sit down* to eat."

"Sorry," said Stephen again.

"Well, just remember that my starter isn't getting any warmer."

"Sorry," said Jenny.

The boy sniffed, as if to say, *Don't do it again*, and moved through to the main room to join the dinner party. Jenny and Stephen heard the words: "Ah! Cyril!" and "How good of you to join us!" and "One minute late though, aren't you?" from inside.

"Cyril seems nice," said Jenny.

"No, he doesn't," said Stephen.

"I was being sarcastic."

"Oh."

"What he really seems like…" said Jenny after a short pause, looking meaningfully at Stephen "…is a boy whose father has taught him that there is only one way to think: *his* way."

Stephen stared at her, then he turned his attention to the dining room where the guests were all seated. Cyril and Trevor McNade were sitting together, smiling smugly as everyone told them how marvellous they both were.

Stephen put his phone away. "Shall we get out of here?" he said to his wife.

PART 2

TIME STOP
6.49pm

That's odd, thought Alfie, looking at his watches both showing the time as 6.49pm. It should have frightened him, but actually it calmed him down. Alfie was so convinced that his watches worked, and couldn't possibly both fail at the same time, that the more likely explanation was that time had stopped. In some way. Which was good news just at the moment, as it meant that he was no longer getting further and further out of step with his routines.

It occurred to him, in fact – as he had

frozen in place with his arms still raised – that if time had stopped he might be stuck, unable to move, which could get very uncomfortable. But, actually, he unfroze his arms and got down from the kitchen table easily.

He wasn't quite sure how best to handle the current situation. But he knew that whatever weirdness was going on was something to do with him saying that he would do exactly what he liked. Not just saying it: shouting it.

And he knew that when he'd said it he'd meant it. In a different way to the way in which Mrs Stokes had been saying it. She had meant: *Yes, dear, you just do whatever. I want to watch* TV. But Alfie, in his anger and frustration, had meant: OK, *I will do what I like* – EXACTLY *what I like* – *just watch me*!

But, when he had shouted it, what he had liked the idea of – what, in other words, he had wanted to happen – was indeed for time to stop.

And that's what *had* happened.

So maybe… maybe…

HAVING-TEA
6.49pm

Alfie sat at the kitchen table again, picked up his knife and fork and said again, loudly: "I'll JUST DO WHAT I LIKE!!"

Since they had just stopped time, he assumed these were magic words. So he expected, on saying them, something magical to happen. But perhaps disappointingly – even though a minute before this was exactly what he had wanted – Mrs Stokes appeared in front of him.

"Oh," he said. "Hello."

"So…" she said. "What would that be?"

"I beg your pardon?" said Alfie.

"What would that be? In this particular case."

"Eh?"

"Oh, come on, Alfie, don't be dense. What – seated as you are at the kitchen table, with your knife, fork and plate at the ready – would you *like* to do?"

Alfie frowned. Not just because he was thinking about answering the question – although he was – but also because he had noticed something about Mrs Stokes. She had come into the room very quickly and was standing up straighter than she had before.

She was speaking to him in a loud, uncrackly voice, without seeming to hear any of *his* words wrong and without her hearing aids feeding back. And her Zimmer frame – if Alfie wasn't mistaken – was *lighting up*. In colour! It was like it had been secretly put together from a batch of different coloured lightsabers – red and blue and yellow and green – and she'd only now switched them on.

"Um…" he said, "I'd *like* to eat some candyfloss."

"OK. Just usual candyfloss or…?"

"I'd like it in the shape of a rocket!"

"Excellent! Now you're getting into the spirit of things! Anything to go with that?"

"Er… chips?"

"Rocket candyfloss and chips!"

Mrs Stokes seemed to concentrate. The colours of her Zimmer frame started flashing. And suddenly there it was, in front of him on the table: a tube of the pinkest, fluffiest candyfloss, shaped exactly like Apollo 13, the rocket ship that Alfie most liked from when they had done the history of the moon landings at school.

The chips were built up next to it, a huge side ladder of them, criss-crossing all the way to the top. It was incredible. Although one weird thing was that beneath the candyfloss rocket there was some mash.

"Er…" said Alfie, prodding at it with his fork, "aren't the chips enough potato?"

"That's smoke!" said Mrs Stokes. "From the lift-off!"

"Brilliant!" said Alfie.

"Anything to drink?" she added. "Perhaps

something that could help power the rocket…?"

"I don't really want to drink oil…"

"No, but it could look a bit like oil…"

Alfie had a thought. "Well, I've always wondered why no one makes a fizzy chocolate drink."

Mrs Stokes clicked her fingers and a glass appeared next to his plate full of something brown, creamy and sparkling.

"Enjoy," she said.

CLEARING-UP-AFTER-TEA
6.49pm

The strange thing about that tea – which might seem, in dietary terms, a little sugary and heavy – is that actually it wasn't. Every bit of the candyfloss rocket that entered Alfie's mouth seemed to change its level of sweetness so that it never became overpowering, the fizzy chocolate went down like a smooth treat and the chips were really light, fluffy and not too greasy.

"It's all organic," said Mrs Stokes, which seemed unlikely in the case of candyfloss, chips and fizzy chocolate, but then again it was *magic* candyfloss, chips and fizzy chocolate, thought Alfie, so there might be a special exemption.

When he'd finished his tea, she said: "What's next?"

"What do you mean?"

"What routine's next?"

"Oh," said Alfie. "Clearing-up-after-tea."

"OK," said Mrs Stokes, "if you were to go about that just as you liked, how would you do it?"

Alfie thought. His first instinct was to say that he wouldn't do it at all, but he felt that would be rude or possibly ungrateful. So he said: "Plates are a bit like flying saucers, aren't they?"

"They are," said Mrs Stokes.

"How do flying saucers fly, Mrs Stokes? They're round and all their jets seem to be underneath, so how do they fly anywhere but upwards?"

"Well," said Mrs Stokes, her face lit by

the flashing Zimmer frame, "they *may* have a propulsion system that creates an anti-gravity effect which curves the jet streams in infinite directions. Or it may just be…" she added, as Alfie's plate floated into the air, "…magic."

The plate hovered in front of Alfie's face, glowing. Then it twirled round.

"Uh-oh…" said Mrs Stokes.

"What?" said Alfie. Mrs Stokes nodded towards the table. The salt-and-pepper shakers were trembling — then they blasted off up towards the plate! Followed closely by a bottle of tomato ketchup, which had also suddenly risen into the air like an enemy rocket ship!

"THE DARK FORCES OF THE CONDIMENT ARE COMING!!"

shouted Mrs Stokes.

Alfie picked up his knife and fork and held them up vertically, like a comic-book picture of a boy expecting food. He levered the knife forward and the fork backwards.

"Go Warp Factor 1! Hyperspeed!!"

The plate zoomed away from his face. Alfie manipulated his knife and fork backwards, forwards and sideways, making the plate zigzag its way through the attacking salt-and-pepper shakers, and enemy-rocket-ship

ketchup. Expertly, he controlled the path of the plate up towards the lampshade, along the dining-room wall and past the canvas photo of him when he was a baby that he wished his parents would take down. (It did occur to him that he could crash the plate into that and destroy it, but he felt that was going too far with doing just what he liked.)

But the shakers and the ketchup speeded up. The condiments were right behind!

"ALFIE!" shouted Mrs Stokes.

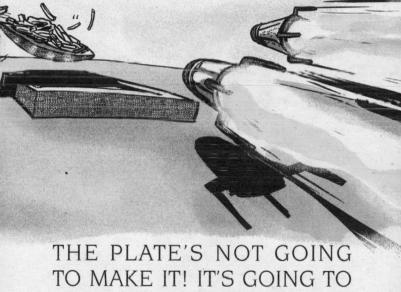

THE PLATE'S NOT GOING TO MAKE IT! IT'S GOING TO GET SALT-AND-PEPPERED! AND... KETCHUP'D!!!"

Alfie knew what to do. He threw his knife and

fork together towards the plate. They whirled round at high speed, like wheels in the air, overtaking the salt-and-pepper shakers, and arcing past the ketchup bottle. Still rotating incredibly fast, they spun themselves on to the side of the plate, giving it that little bit of extra speed it needed… to get to the dishwasher!

Which Mrs Stokes opened just in time for the plate, knife and fork to separate and drop into the right parts of the rack.

"Fabulous," she said. "What about your glass?"

"I think I'm OK just to bring that over," said Alfie.

HOMEWORK
6.49pm

Alfie looked at the book he was meant to read. It was big, heavy and called *Marine Biology: An Introduction*.

"Can we just make this one disappear?" said Alfie.

"Yes, why not?" said Mrs Stokes, picking it up. "You'll probably find out what you need to know about this somewhere or other anyway."

With that, she put the book down and walked through to the living room.

"Hang on!" said Alfie, following her. "Isn't the book actually going to disappear?"

"Well, it has, hasn't it?" said Mrs Stokes, looking around. "I can't see it. Now what?" she added, looking down at a copy of the routines she was holding. "Ah! My favourite!"

She picked up the remote control and switched on the TV.

LIMITED-AMOUNT-OF-TV
6.49pm

The Simpsons was on. It was a funny episode –
the one in which Grampa Simpson turns out
to have been a professional wrestler – but
after all the excitement involved in having
and clearing up tea in the way Alfie had just
done, just sitting there and watching TV felt
a little... well, for want of a better word...
routine.

"So," said Mrs Stokes, "are you doing *just
what you like*?"

"Well, yes..." said Alfie. "But now it feels
like I want *more*."

"Ah," said the old lady. "That's what happens, you see, Alfie, when we get just what we like. Appetite grows. It spirals. The more you're allowed to do exactly what you want, the more you *need* – to satisfy the need *inside*."

"Oh, I see," said Alfie, nodding. "So... this whole experience is, like, teaching me that? About always wanting more and more stuff? Will the next magic thing that happens get out of control and I'll nearly die, but at least I'll have learnt an important life lesson?"

"Nah," said Mrs Stokes.

"Oh, OK," said Alfie. "In that case, I'd like to go into the TV."

And the next thing he knew he was. A yellow, three-fingered version of himself was at the side of the wrestling ring, shouting at Grampa Simpson. Then the channel changed – because Alfie wanted it to, and also because Mrs Stokes had provided him with a remote control to take into the TV. Alfie was now on Cartoon Network in an episode of his favourite show, *The Amazing World of Gumball*. He was a kind of half-frog, half-apple jumping around at Elmore Junior High School.

Unlike *The Simpsons*, this wasn't an episode that had actually been on TV; it just followed a story that Alfie made up as he went along, where Gumball and Darwin were in competition to be his best friend (it ended up with them fighting each other with jelly-and-custard guns and Alfie deciding it was a draw).

Then Alfie pressed another button on his remote control. Some very dramatic music started playing and he found himself in a dark suit and tie, reading the seven o'clock news.

Oh dear, he thought, *wrong button*, as a man poked his head round from behind a camera, looking very, very confused. *Still, might as well make the most of it.*

"Good evening," said Alfie, "this is the seven o'clock news. All children between the ages of seven and twelve are allowed not to go to school tomorrow. Broccoli Bake has been outlawed. And Freddie Barnes, of 14 Brackenbury Road, is from this moment on to be officially known as Freddie 'Bum-Bum' Barnes. Goodnight!"

And the dramatic theme music started again.

BA-BA-BA BA-BA!

BONG! BO-BO-BONG!

BA! BA!

BA-BA!

BATH
6.49pm

Alfie came out of the TV, still wearing the suit and tie.

"You weren't in there very long," said Mrs Stokes.

Alfie shrugged. "It's a limited-amount-of-TV. Always."

"Of course. Why have you kept the suit on?"

"I've got an idea," he said. "For bathtime."

"Ah. Looking forward to it," she replied.

When they reached the bathroom – which was on the second floor, and Mrs Stokes seemed to get up there as quickly as Alfie, two steps at a time – he said: "I'm thinking the suit and tie could change into… a frogman's outfit!"

"Fabulous!"

"And then the bath…"

"Just dive in, Alfie," she said.

He did. The suit and tie became a scuba-diving suit and he dived down and down into the bath. Deeper and deeper he went, passing schools of fish and lobsters and whales, before meeting a dolphin, which was standing on its tail underwater, like they sometimes do.

"Hi, Alfie," said the dolphin. "I'm Dolph."

"As in Lundgren?" said Alfie.

"How have you heard of *him*?" said Dolph.

"My dad's a big fan of his old films."

"Right. Well, no. Dolph as in dolphin."

"I see," said Alfie. "How come you can hear what I'm saying underwater?"

"Well," said Dolph, "there are a number of things to consider there. Firstly, in normal scuba-diving, you're not allowed to take the breathing apparatus out of your mouth, which means you can't speak at all. Secondly, I'm a talking dolphin. Called Dolph. So, y'know, let's not worry about it."

"OK," said Alfie.

"Who's the old dear?" said Dolph.

Alfie looked round. Mrs Stokes was floating down towards him. Out of the ends of the legs of her Zimmer frame, which was still lit up, he could see bubbles rushing towards the surface of the water, as if jet-propelled.

"Hello!" she said. "I thought I'd join you for this one. Test out the Zimmer's amphibious capability."

"Great," said Alfie. "But I'm not sure about the new trousers."

"They're not trousers," she said, "they're scales. And a tail. I've gone the full mermaid."

"I see," said Alfie, relieved that she hadn't gone the full, *full* mermaid – above her waist she was still wearing her green if-the-Queen-shopped-at-Oxfam top and pearls. *And* carrying her handbag.

"Are you two coming?" said Dolph. "I haven't got all day."

So Alfie and Mrs Stokes swam after Dolph along the bath bottom, which wasn't white and enamel and one-metre long, but covered with coral and infinite. They swam through schools of zigzagging clownfish and crawling lobsters and floating turtles; they hovered above the bright pink and blue coral, speckled by reflected sunlight, out of which long and slinky moray eels peered to look at them; they saw, far beneath them, underwater cities with curly, far-reaching spires and underwater caves where lost treasure sparkled in open ancient, moss-covered chests.

And they also – bit of a bonus – found an old rubber duck bath toy that Alfie thought he'd lost ages ago.

Then, suddenly, they were attacked by a school of sharks, approaching in a terrifying V-formation!

"Oh no!" said Alfie. "Is *this* the bit where I nearly die, but learn my lesson?"

"Nah," said Mrs Stokes. She brought her

thumbs and forefingers up to her ears and made a couple of small adjustments. The next thing Alfie knew, a huge piercing wail of feedback was powering out of her hearing aids. The sharks' V-formation fell apart, as they retreated as fast as possible, terrified.

"Thanks, Mrs Stokes," said Alfie.

"Yeah, thanks," said Dolph.

"Pardon?" said Mrs Stokes.

CLEANING-HIS-TEETH-IN-THE-EVENING
6.49pm

"So," said Alfie, toothbrush in hand, after he and Mrs Stokes had towelled themselves dry and let the bathwater out, "I think the key thing with *this* one is making it different, for once, from the morning version."

"Hmm," said Mrs Stokes. "How are we going to do that?"

"Can I help?"

They turned round. Standing there, in front of the bath, was Dolph.

"Are you OK to be out of the water?" said Alfie.

"Yes. I'm a mammal, not a fish. I don't have gills. I breathe air just like you, only out of my blowhole." Dolph bent his head and puffed towards Alfie, who felt the – slightly fishy – breath on his face. "As long as I keep my skin damp, I'm OK."

"You see," said Mrs Stokes to Alfie, "you've done your marine biology homework after all."

"Yes, thanks, Dolph," said Alfie. "But meanwhile: teeth?"

"Well, what I do is open my enormous mouth, let loads of little plankton swim inside and they feed on my teeth, cleaning them at the same time."

"Right…" said Alfie.

"I'm sensing you don't fancy that much, Alfie," said Mrs Stokes.

"Really?" said Dolph. "I love it. They do a great job and it tickles. In a nice way."

"Maybe this is different enough," said Alfie, squeezing the toothpaste on to his brush.

"How do you mean?" said Mrs Stokes.

"Well, in the morning, I never have a talking dolphin in here when I'm cleaning my teeth."

"Good point."

So he started brushing his teeth. Just for good measure, Mrs Stokes and Dolph joined hands – well, hands and fins – and did a dance, an exact copy of one that Mrs Stokes had just watched on *Strictly* – the American Smooth – to the rhythm of his brush strokes. Just to make sure this teeth-clean was *very* different.

GETTING-UNDRESSED-AND-PUTTING-PYJAMAS-ON
6.49pm

"Let's do this one quickly, Mrs Stokes!" said Alfie, as they went into his bedroom.

"No sooner said than done!"

And the next thing Alfie knew, his clothes had disappeared into the wardrobe and his pyjamas were on.

(There was no nakedness in between, in case you were worried.)

GOING-TO-BED
6.49pm

Alfie lay in bed, looking up at Mrs Stokes and Dolph.

"It's probably time to go to sleep now, Alfie," said Mrs Stokes."

Alfie checked his two watches.

"It isn't actually. It's still 6.49."

"Well. Firstly, your watches might be wrong... don't make that 'they never are' face, Alfie, they *might* be. Secondly, you've done all your routines and thirdly, I'm still your babysitter, and the most important job of a babysitter is to make sure you don't exhaust yourself and be too tired to get up the next morning."

"Is that right?" said Dolph. "I'd say the most important job of a babysitter is to make sure the child they're looking after doesn't die."

Mrs Stokes gave him a look that Alfie could tell meant: *I will not be lectured about babysitting by a dolphin, talking or not*. Alfie wasn't sure whether Dolph would be able to pick up that kind of unspoken message, but he looked away and went *clickclickclickclickclickclick* in what seemed like a told-off manner.

"But," said Alfie, "I've just remembered one more routine!"

"Really?" said Mrs Stokes, opening her handbag and getting out all the pieces of paper from the walls.

"Have you had those with you the whole time?"

"Yes," she said, flicking through them one by one. "Got to make sure you stick to them." She looked up. "But there isn't another routine. Going-to-bed is the last one."

"No, it's not one I normally do. It's not even one that my dad set up for me. It's one that Freddie Barnes told me he does every night, secretly, when he goes to bed…"

Mrs Stokes frowned. "I thought we didn't like Freddie Barnes?"

"Yeah," said Dolph, "I heard he calls you Boring, Boring—"

"Yes, we're all aware of that," said Mrs Stokes.

"Well," said Alfie, "it's more of a game, really that he made up than a routine. But he told me he does do it every night, so I guess it does count as one."

"Right…"

"Well, I always kind of wanted to try it. But I never did."

Mrs Stokes shrugged. "OK. What does Freddie Barnes's secret, naughty routine involve, Alfie?"

Alfie smiled, turned his whole body round and dived down under the bedclothes.

Down he went, down and down, even further than he'd gone into the bath. The sheets ballooned around him, as he slid into the depths of the bed. He was joined about halfway down by Mrs Stokes and Dolph.

"Wheeee!" said Mrs Stokes.

"Wheee!" said Dolph.

Alfie took this to mean that they'd forgotten their differences.

"SO WHAT HAPPENS, ALFIE?" shouted Mrs Stokes.

"YOU HAVE TO GET TO THE BOTTOM OF THE BED, TURN YOUR BODY ROUND AND THEN GET BACK OUT TO THE TOP BEFORE THE ENEMY CAN GET YOU!"

As he shouted this back at her, the three

of them dropped out of the enormous tunnel of cotton on to some concrete. They landed on their feet, except for Dolph, who landed on his tummy. Mrs Stokes looked around. They appeared to be in the darkly lit streets of a seaside town, near the water.

"Where are we, Alfie?" she said.

"Well, I think it's like… the war."

"Yes, I thought it felt familiar. So…" She rubbed her hands with excitement and looked from side to side. "Who's the enemy? Germans? Viet Cong? Al-Qaeda?"

"No…"

"What's that smell?" said Dolph.

Mrs Stokes looked up and sniffed. "Yes. What is that?"

"That's the bit I haven't told you," said Alfie. "That's what makes it fun! That's why it's called… ESCAPE FROM FARTY HARBOUR!!"

Mrs Stokes and Dolph looked at him.

"Right," she said eventually. "So, if I

understand you correctly, Alfie, what you're saying is that you *let one go* just now? Before we all dived into the bed?"

"Yes. That's what Freddie told me you have to do. I kept it in specially until the right moment."

Mrs Stokes and Dolph looked at each other.

"Er…" said Dolph. "You know I was explaining just now about how I breathe air just like you, only through my blowhole?"

"Yes?"

He nodded his head towards the town. A huge green gas cloud was billowing over the rooftops, coming straight towards them.

"I wish I didn't," said Dolph.

As he said this, many people came staggering down the streets, choking and fainting and crying for help.

"OH MY GOD!" shouted Mrs Stokes. "RUN FOR IT!"

"ESCAPE FROM FARTY HARBOUR!" shouted Alfie enthusiastically.

"Yes!" said Mrs Stokes. "Let's very much hope we can!"

"It's been nice knowing you!" said Dolph, and then he dived into the sea.

Mrs Stokes and Alfie ran along the seafront, splashed a little by the water coming off Dolph's escape dive. But it was windy, as it often is by the sea, even by a sea at the bottom of an eleven-year-old boy's bed, and the terrifying green cloud was catching up with them.

"COME ON, MRS STOKES!" shouted Alfie.

"I'M GOING AS FAST AS I CAN! I'M AN OLD WOMAN!"

"BUT YOU'RE A MAGIC OLD WOMAN!"

"I'M NOT *THAT* MAGIC!!" she said in between great panting breaths.

She was slowing down and starting to hobble along. In fact, as Alfie stared back at her, he realised she was looking more like she

had done when she'd first arrived at his house.

He stopped running and took her hand.

"IT'S NO GOOD, ALFIE!"
"NO, COME ON, YOU'LL BE FINE!"

But, even as he said it, his nose twitched and he realised it was too late: they had been enveloped by the terrible cloud.

"Actually, I don't think it smells that bad…" said Alfie.

"Of course you don't!" said Mrs Stokes. "No one thinks their own ones do! But I… *urrgggghhh*!!!"

She coughed, spluttered and fell to the ground.

"MRS STOKES!" shouted Alfie.
"HOLD YOUR BREATH!"

"I can't, dear," she whispered weakly. "I hardly have any breath at the best of times…"

Her eyes began closing. The green cloud became thicker and smellier. Even Alfie now felt he didn't want to breathe it in. *That's the last time I eat candyfloss rocket and chips*, he thought. *And as for fizzy chocolate…*

"Mrs Stokes! Mrs Stokes! Is *this* the time things get out of control and I nearly die, but learn my lesson?!"

"Nah," said Mrs Stokes.

"Oh good."

"I think it's the time things get of control and *I* nearly die," she said.

"No, Mrs Stokes! No!"

"It's OK, Alfie," she said. "Well, it's not OK, it's absolutely disgusting. But I mean it's OK to leave me. I'm an old woman."

"But you're a magic old woman!"

"You said that before. And as I said at the time – it was only about two minutes ago so I don't know why I'm having to repeat myself so soon – I'm not *that* magic. And now, I'm afraid, the overwhelming stinkiness of your fart has taken away all that's left… of my magic… Save yourself, Alfie. Save yourself!"

With that, her eyes closed. The green cloud thickened even more around them. Alfie felt the rising panic – the feeling that had first appeared when Mrs Stokes had been saying *just do what you like* over and over again – returning. He wished he hadn't gone off-piste with one of Freddie Barnes's stupid routines. *Of course* that was going to create trouble. He should just have stuck, like his dad had told him, to his *own* routines.

That thought, though, gave him an idea.

The post-school routines were designed to make sure he was in bed at an appropriate time every night, so that he got a good eleven hours' sleep. That was why he had never done ESCAPE FROM FARTY HARBOUR before, even though it sounded like fun. It was part of his bedtime routine to be asleep by 8.35pm on weekdays and 9.35pm on weekends. It was, in some ways, the most *essential* part of all his routines.

And if there was one thing Alfie was good

at, it was following his routines. Even tonight with Mrs Stokes, although they'd been very different from normal, he'd still done each routine, one after the other, in the same pattern as usual. Until this last one.

So he said: "Hold on Mrs Stokes! Hold on!" And raised both his arms, and stared at his watches, and thought hard, as hard as he'd ever thought, about being back in bed, and fast asleep, by 9.35pm (because today was Saturday – obviously – *Strictly* was on). He made the numbers 9, 3 and 5 (with one dot after the 9) bigger than big, painting them inside his brain like a graffiti artist, until there was nothing, not one thing, in Alfie Moore's mind at all except:

9.35pm

…and an image of himself asleep, as normal, with the watches on his wrists showing that time.

PART 3

CHAPTER 7
10.25pm

"That's really strange, isn't it?"

"Yes. Really strange."

"Why would she send a text like that?"

Alfie stirred, opening his eyes just a little. Through the mist of sleep, he could see his parents standing by his bed, whispering. Although not whispering quite quietly enough, as it had woken him up. Or at least, half woken him up.

"Oh sorry, Alfie!" said Jenny. "We just came in to check on you."

"I'm fine," said Alfie. "What time is it?"

"It's 10.25…" said Stephen.

Alfie sat up in bed. "You're back early."

Stephen and Jenny glanced at each other.

"Yes… well," said Jenny. "We kind of decided… not to stay too long at the dinner party."

"Oh. What did you do instead?"

Stephen and Jenny's glance became a smile.

"We… went for a walk. In the park," Stephen said.

"A walk," said Jenny, looking lovingly at her husband. "And a run. And a tree-climb. And a dance."

"The park? But it's shut…"

"Yes. We climbed over the fence," said Jenny, her smile widening.

"Jenny! Don't tell him tha—"

"Anyway, time to go back to sleep. We shouldn't have woken you up. Not after you did so well getting to bed at 9.35 like we asked."

"Yes, well… I stuck to all my routines. I did, Dad."

"Did you? Oh…" said Stephen. "Well. That's great, Alfie. But me and Jenny were talking on the way back tonight and we thought maybe we should… loosen up a bit with the routines. I mean, it's good to have *some*, but maybe… maybe it's fine not to worry about sticking to them *all* the time."

Alfie thought about this. But not for very long, as he was really sleepy.

"OK," he said, settling back down under the covers. "By the way, I had the most amazing dream tonight."

"Did you?" said Jenny, surprised.

"Really?" said Stephen.

"Yes. It was fantastic. Mrs Stokes was in it!"

"Oh!"

"Yes. I like her. She's a great babysitter…"

Jenny and his dad exchanged glances again, clearly surprised.

"Oh good!" said Jenny.

"Can I have her again soon?"

"Well… yes. I guess. Depends how long Stasia's mum takes to recover from the pig accident…"

"Have you kept her phone number…?"

"Yes," said his dad and took out the yellowing card with the flowers on it. He held it up and stared at it again. Alfie, even through his sleepiness, could make out the words on the back.

"Dad…" said Alfie, "where did we get the number from? Who wrote that on the back of the card?"

His dad and Jenny looked at each other. Jenny seemed a little bit uncertain, but then nodded.

"Your mum, Alfie," his dad said. "It must have been. It's her handwriting. Mrs Stokes must have been her babysitter when *she* was young. It's odd, though. I don't remember her ever suggesting we use her when…"

"When she was alive," said Alfie.

"Yes," said his dad.

"I suppose she must have written it and put it in that drawer for us to find." Alfie paused. He could feel sleep coming. *In case of emergencies.*

His dad looked at the card. Then he looked at Alfie. His eyes were a little moist. "I suppose she must."

Alfie yawned and shut his eyes. "Where's Mrs Stokes by the way...?" A scary memory from his dream came back to him of Mrs Stokes collapsing. From fart poisoning.

"Oh," replied Jenny, "she's just leaving. It's a bit difficult for her to come up the stairs, I think."

Oh good, thought Alfie. *She's OK. But of course she is. It was just a dream.*

"Hang on..." said Stephen. He went out on to the landing and called down. "MRS STOKES! MRS STOKES! I'LL

BE THERE IN A MOMENT
TO SEE YOU OUT!"
"NO NEED FOR TROUT!"
called up Mrs Stokes, her voice crackly again.
"I've already eaten!"

Alfie smiled and turned over. Through the
cotton of his pillow, he heard the *ting* of a text
coming into Jenny's phone.

"Not *another* one from Freddie Barnes's
mum!" she said.

"For heaven's sake," came his dad's voice
from the landing. "I mean, it's not Alfie's
fault that people call her son 'Bum-Bum'. Is
it?"

"Well, she says it is. She says... hold on... *Alfie
told everyone to say it on the news*. On the news?!!!"

"Must be a misprint. Autocorrect. Or she's
just completely gone mad."

That was when Alfie really started to go to
sleep. But the smile stayed on his face.

"MRS STOKES!" shouted Alfie's dad again. "Oh, the old dear hasn't heard me. MRS STOKES!"

"YES, DEAR!" Her voice sailed up from downstairs.

"WE'LL JUST COME DOWN AND SEE YOU OUT!"

There was a short pause. Then, not-crackly but loud and clear and coming up the stairs like a rocket, or a rush of air from a dolphin's blowhole, the words:

"JUST DO WHAT YOU LIKE!"

And, with that, Alfie Moore fell fast asleep.

"I wish I had better parents!" Barry said, a third time. And then suddenly the entire room started to shake…

Barry Bennett hates being called Barry. In fact it's number 2 on the list of things he blames his parents for, along with 1) 'being boring' and 3) 'always being tired'.

But there is a world, not far from this one, where parents don't just *have* children… In this world, children are allowed to *choose* their parents.

For Barry, this seems like a dream come true, only things turn out to be not quite that simple…

Fred and Ellie are twins. But not identical (because that's impossible for a boy and a girl). They do like all the same things, though. Especially video games. Which they are very good at. They aren't *that* good, however, at much else – like, for example, football, or dealing with the school bullies.

Then they meet the Mystery man, who sends them a video game controller, which doesn't look like any other controller they've ever seen. And it doesn't control any of their usual games. When the twins find out what it *does* control though, it seems like the answer to all their problems. At least it *seems* like that…

Go on another crazy adventure with
a hapless hero who bites off more than
he can chew in…

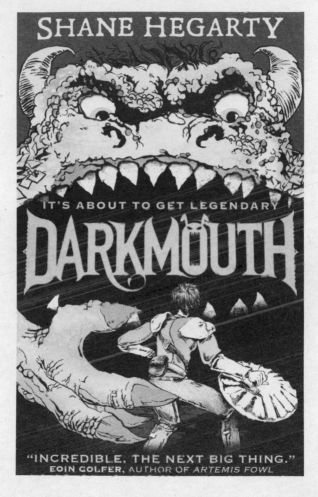

SHANE HEGARTY

IT'S ABOUT TO GET LEGENDARY

DARKMOUTH

"INCREDIBLE. THE NEXT BIG THING."
EOIN COLFER, AUTHOR OF *ARTEMIS FOWL*

Turn the page to read an extract.

I

The town of Darkmouth appears on few maps because very few people want to find it. When it is marked on one, its location is always wrong. It'll be a bit north of where it's supposed to be, or a bit south. A little left or a little right. A bit off.

Always.

Which means that visitors to Darkmouth invariably arrive having taken a wrong turn, soon convinced they'll reach only a dead end. They drive through a canopy of trees, whose branches reach from either side to clasp ever tighter overhead, becoming thicker with every mile until the dappled light is choked off and the road is dark even on the brightest of days. Then, just as the wood is almost scraping the paint from their car, and it seems that the road itself is going to be suffocated, the visitors travel through a short tunnel and emerge on to a roundabout filled with blossoming flowers and featuring a sign that reads:

The next line has been updated by hand a couple of times:

On a wall lining the road there is large striking graffiti. It says only this:

Except the last S forms a serpent, with mouth wide and teeth jagged. Visitors peer at it and wonder, *Is that a…? Could it be a…?*

Yes, that snake really *is* swallowing a child.

The travellers – by now a bit desperate in their search – have finally reached Darkmouth. Their next thought is this: *Let's get out of here.*

So they go right round the roundabout and head back the way they came. Which is a shame, because if they were to stay they would realise that Darkmouth is actually quite a nice little place. It has a colourful little ice-cream shop on the harbour, benches dotted along the strand, picnic tables and fun climbing frames for the kids.

And no one has been eaten by a monster for some time.

In fact, they aren't really monsters at all. They might *look* monstrous, and the locals might refer to them as monsters, but, strictly speaking, they are Legends. Myths. Fables.

They once shared the Earth with humans, only to grow envious, then violent, so that a war raged through the world's Blighted Villages for centuries.

Now Darkmouth is the last of these Blighted Villages. And Legends show up only occasionally.

This morning just happens to be one of those occasions.

2

Thinking back on it all later, Finn identified that morning as the time when things began to go badly wrong. Thinking on it a little bit *more*, he realised he could identify just about any morning of his first twelve years as when things began to go wrong. At the time, though, he wasn't doing much thinking. Instead, he was running. As hard as he could. In a clanking armoured suit and heavy helmet. In the rain. Away from a Minotaur.

Five minutes earlier, everything had *seemed* to be going a bit more to plan, even if Finn wasn't entirely sure what that plan was.

Then it had been Finn doing the chasing, carrying a Desiccator, a fat silver rifle with a

Desiccator

cylinder hanging in front of the trigger. He was the Hunter, lumbering through the maze of Darkmouth's backstreets in a black helmet and fighting suit – small dull squares of metal knitted together clumsily – so that when he moved it sounded like a bag of forks falling downstairs.

It was oversized because his parents had told him he should leave room to grow into it. It rattled because he had made it himself.

From somewhere in the near distance, about two laneways away, he had heard the sound of glass being mashed into stone, or maybe stone being pounded into glass. Either way, it was followed by the scream of a car alarm and the even louder scream of a person.

Darkmouth was a town of dead ends and blind alleys, with high walls that were lined with broken glass, sharp stones and blades. The layout was designed to confuse Legends, block their progress, shepherd them towards dead ends. But Finn knew where to go.

He followed the Legend's dusty trail, emerging on to Broken Road, Darkmouth's main street, where vehicles had screeched to a halt at wrong angles, and those townspeople who hadn't scarpered were cowering in still-closed shop doorways.

And at the top of the street, glancing over its shoulder, was the Minotaur. It was part human, part bull, all terrifying. Finn's heart skipped a beat, hammered three more in quick succession. He took a shuddering breath. He had spent his childhood looking at drawings of such creatures, which were always depicted as mighty, almost noble, Legends. Seeing one in the flesh, Finn realised they had captured its strength, but had not really conveyed any sense of just how rabid it looked.

From where its jutting, crooked horns met its great bull's head, it was covered in the mangy hair of a mongrel. As it looked back, slobber dripped from its great teeth and ran through the contours of muscles bulging along its back, past its waist down to patches of skin as cracked as baked clay. It stood on two legs that tapered down to menacing claws instead of hooves.

The Minotaur was worse than Finn had ever imagined it could be. And he had imagined it to be pretty bad.

It was looking straight at him.

He ducked into a doorway. A woman was already hiding there, her back pressed against the door, a dog pulled close. Her face was tight with fear.

"Don't worry, Mrs Bright," Finn told her, his voice muffled by the helmet. "You and Yappy will soon be safe, won't you, boy?" He petted the dog, a basset hound, with his free hand. It sneezed on him.

The woman nodded with unconvincing gratitude, then paused. "Where's your father, young man? Shouldn't he be—?"

There was a smash further up the street. The Minotaur had disappeared round the turn at the top of Broken Road. Finn took another deep breath and moved on after it.

From the other side of a wall, there was a thud so forceful it sent a shudder from Finn's feet to his brain, which interpreted it as a signal to run screaming in the opposite direction.

But Finn didn't run. He had trained for this. He had been born into it. He knew what was expected of him, what he needed to do. Besides, if he ran now, his dad would be disappointed in him. Again.

I'll be there when you need me, Finn's father had told him that morning.

Pressing a radio button on the side of his helmet, Finn whispered, "Dad? Are you there?"

The only response was the uncaring crackle of static.

A dark, looming hulk crossed an intersecting laneway, tearing along its narrow walls. Finn raised his Desiccator and followed. At the corner, he crouched and peered round. The Minotaur had paused no more than twenty metres away. Its great shoulders heaved under angry, growling breaths as it figured out which way to go next.

It was all up to Finn now. He recalled his training. Focused on what he had been taught. Thought about his father's expert words. Carefully, he aimed his stocky silver weapon, steadied himself, exhaled.

At that exact moment, the Minotaur turned to face him, its eyes like black pools gouged beneath scarred horns. Froth dripped from chipped and jagged tusks. For a second, Finn was distracted by the way drool, blood and rain clung to a crystal ring wedged through the Legend's nose.

The Minotaur roared.

Finn squeezed the trigger.

The force of the shot sent Finn tripping backwards. A sparkling, spinning blue ball flew from the barrel of the Desiccator, unfurling into a glowing net as it was propelled towards where the Minotaur had stood only a moment before… and wrapped itself

Minotaur

round a parked car.

Finn groaned.

With a flash and a stifled *whooop*, half the car collapsed in on itself with the anguished scrunch of a ton of metal being sucked into a shape no bigger than a soda can.

Finn looked for the Minotaur. It was gone.

He pressed his radio switch. "Erm, Dad?"

Still nothing.

He paused, calmed his babbling mind as much as he could and moved off again through the laneways. Using the ancient methods handed down to him, Finn began carefully tracking the trail of the Minotaur.

He needn't have bothered. The Minotaur got to him first.

WORLD BOOK DAY *fest*

WORLD **BOOK** DAY
3 MARCH 2016

Want to **READ** more?

VISIT YOUR LOCAL BOOKSHOP

- Get some great recommendations for what to read next

- Meet your favourite authors & illustrators at brilliant events

- Discover books you never even knew existed!

FIND YOUR LOCAL BOOKSHOP
www.booksellers.org.uk/ bookshopsearch

JOIN YOUR LOCAL LIBRARY

You can browse and borrow from a HUGE selection of books and get recommendations of what to read next from expert librarians— all for **FREE**! You can also discover libraries' wonderful children's and family reading activities.

FIND YOUR LOCAL LIBRARY
www.findalibrary.co.uk

GET

ONLINE

VISIT **WORLDBOOKDAY.COM** TO DISCOVER A WHOLE NEW WORLD OF BOOKS!

- Downloads and activities for top books and authors
- Cool games, trailers and videos
- Author events in your area
- News, competitions and new books—all in a FREE monthly email

AND MORE!